Lily and the Magical Moonbeam

For Gillian and Reinis
S.G.

ORCHARD BOOKS
96 Leonard Street, London EC2A 4XD
Orchard Books Australia
32/45-51 Huntley Street, Alexandria, NSW 2015
First published in Great Britain in 2003
First paperback publication in 2004
ISBN 1 84121 466 3 (hardback)
ISBN 1 84362 289 0 (paperback)
Text and illustrations © Stephen Gulbis 2003
The right of Stephen Gulbis to be identified as the author
and illustrator of this work has been asserted by him in accordance
with the Copyright, Designs and Patents Act, 1988.
A CIP catalogue record for this book is available from the British Library.
(hardback) 10 9 8 7 6 5 4 3 2 1
(paperback) 10 9 8 7 6 5 4 3 2 1
Printed in Hong Kong, China

Lily and the Magical Moonbeam

Stephen Gulbis

ORCHARD BOOKS

Perched on a rocky reef, beside the salty sea, stood a lighthouse. Inside lived Lily the lighthouse keeper and her little dog, Angus.

Looking after the lighthouse was busy work. Every day, Lily skipped up and down the tower.

"Polish the lamp," she huffed.

"Sound the foghorn,"
she puffed.

"Feed the seagulls,"
she panted.
"Woof! Woof!"
barked Angus.

When darkness fell, Lily turned
on the lighthouse lamp to guide the
fishing boats around the rocky reef.

One dark night, when the wind howled around the lighthouse, Lily heard a SPLASH! "Help!" cried a little voice. Lily threw a lifebelt into the waves and pulled it hard. There, all shivering and wet, lay a poor, soggy creature.

"Who are you?" asked Lily.
"I'm a magical moonbeam,"
croaked a tiny voice. "The wind was so
strong that it blew me out of the sky."

Angus fetched a soft, fluffy towel.
"Don't worry, you're safe now,
little moonbeam," Lily said, and
the moonbeam began to glow.

When it grew dark, Lily and the
moonbeam turned on the lighthouse lamp.
   "What a lovely night!" said Lily.
"Look at all those stars."
   "They're my twinkly friends," smiled the
moonbeam, and he remembered how
he used to glisten and glow beside them.

Lily loved having the magical moonbeam in the lighthouse. She had moonlit suppers . . .

and moonlit baths, and at bedtime the moonbeam glowed above her pillow.

The magical moonbeam loved being with Lily, too.
But every now and then, he would gaze up
into the night sky and think of home.

One day, Lily noticed that the moonbeam
wasn't glowing as brightly as usual.
   "What's the matter?" Lily asked.
   "I miss my friends," said the moonbeam, sadly.
"I think it's time I went home."
Lily didn't want to say goodbye.
   "Please stay a little longer," she said.

But the magical moonbeam's light was beginning to flicker and fade. Lily knew that she had to do something. But how could she help her friend?

"Woof! Woof!" barked Angus.
He had spotted some seagulls.
  "Good idea, Angus," said Lily.
"Can you help us?" Lily called to the
seagulls. But with a screech and a
squawk they skimmed out of sight.

Lily looked down at the moonbeam.
His last little glimmer had almost gone.
"My poor magical moonbeam," she whispered.
Just then Lily heard something . . .

Screeching and squawking, a whole
flock of seagulls swooped down to the rescue!
Gently Lily put the moonbeam into her bucket.
"Goodbye my little moonbeam," she said softly.
Then the seagulls lifted the moonbeam up into the starry sky.
Higher and higher they flew, until at last, the magical
moonbeam was back with his twinkly friends.

Lily missed having her magical friend in the lighthouse. Slowly, she trudged up and down the tower. Polish the lamp . . .

sound the foghorn . . .

feed the seagulls.

That night a great storm raged around the rocky reef.
The whistling wind and crashing waves kept Lily awake.
"If only my magical moonbeam was here,"
she thought, when suddenly. . .

. . . the lighthouse went dark!
"Oh no!" cried Lily. "The lamp's broken.
Now the fishing boats are in danger!"
In the darkness she hugged Angus tightly,
"What are we going to do?"

All at once, the darkness vanished
and a bright light swept over the sea.
Above the lighthouse, glowing
brighter than ever, shone Lily's
magical moonbeam!

"Woof! Woof!" barked Angus.

"Now everyone's safe!" cried Lily.
"Thank you magical moonbeam."
The moonbeam glowed brighter still.
"You're welcome," he said.
"That's what friends are for!"

At last the storm blew over and Lily snuggled down in her bed.

"Goodnight Angus, goodnight magical moonbeam," she whispered.

"Goodnight Lily," said the moonbeam softly, as Lily fell fast asleep.